DREAMING IN BLACK & WHITE

DREAMING IN BLACK & WHITE

Reinhardt Jung

Translated by Anthea Bell

Phyllis Fogelman Books

New York

First published in the United States 2003
by Phyllis Fogelman Books
A division of Penguin Young Readers Group
345 Hudson Street, New York, New York 10014
First published in Germany 1996 by Verlag Jungbrunnen
German title: *Auszeit oder Der Löwe von Kauba*
First published in Great Britain 2000 by Mammoth,
an imprint of Egmont Children's Books Limited
Text copyright © 1996 by Verlag Jungbrunnen Wien München
Translation copyright © 2000 by Egmont Children's Books Limited
All rights reserved
Designed by Jasmin Rubero
Text set in Goudy
Printed in the U.S.A. on acid-free paper

1 3 5 7 9 10 8 6 4 2

Library of Congress Cataloging-in-Publication Data
Jung, Reinhardt, date.
[Auszeit. English]
Dreaming in black & white / Reinhardt Jung ;
translated by Anthea Bell.
p.   cm.
Originally published under the title:
Auszeit oder Der Löwe von Kauba. Wien : Jungbrunnen, 1996.
Summary: A physically handicapped boy dreams
that he is a student during the period of
the Nazi Third Reich in Germany,
where he is persecuted for being crippled.
ISBN 0-8037-2811-5
1. Germany—History—1933–1945—Juvenile fiction.
[1. Germany—History—1933–1945—Fiction.
2. People with disabilities—Fiction.] I. Bell, Anthea. II. Title.
PZ7.J955 Dr 2003
[Fic]—dc21   2002019918

CONTENTS

DREAMING
IN BLACK
&
WHITE

CHAPTER ONE

The collected album of photos was among Great-Grandpa's things. It's called *Adventures in German South-West Africa,* and there's a picture of a lion in it. The lion is injured. When I look at him hard, it gives me goose bumps. I can't be sure whether it's me looking at him or him staring back at me out of the picture. I wonder who took the photo of that lion. What happens when you take a photograph? The picture captures a moment. Well, it really captures light, so it must have torn a hole in the light somewhere. It's taking light away.

When I was little, I didn't like being photographed. It scared me. The picture takes something away from you, freezing a moment in time. There should be shadows behind every photo, but there aren't. All the same, photos are shadows coming out of the past and into my eyes.

An injured lion is dangerous.

Not in the picture, but in my head.

The photo's black and white.

Normally a lion is the color of dry grass, yellowish, tawny. But this one is black and white.

He's been dead a long time now.

I'm glad I'm living today. If I'd lived *back*

then, I'd be a survivor now. Or maybe I wouldn't. *Back then*, people like me were supposed to be dead. Ours were lives not worth living. Even as it is, I'm really a survivor: I survived my birth. Which you can't always take for granted. Some parents don't want to carry the burden, and some doctors know it.

I'm alive.

Although I oughtn't to be, not in view of genetic engineering. I'm not the way anyone would actually want to be. All the same, I often think I'm lucky, because I really like being alive!

Sometimes I wonder if I was ever on this earth before. So many things strike me as familiar.

Including the lion.

There's a reproachful look in his eyes. It's not me he's reproaching: I'm one hundred percent against lion hunting!

I'm against keeping lions in cages too.

My parents say I have too much imagination. Imagination is when you can be in two places at once; here and there at the same time, yesterday and today both together. Then I don't know for sure where I really am. My parents say I dream too much. They think the things I dream aren't real, but in my dream, everything I'm dreaming is real to me. When I wake up, it always takes me a little while to adjust to the real world again. Because it seems so unreal after my dream.

Mother thinks I have these dreams because we're studying "those terrible times" in school at the moment.

Personally, I think it's something inside me.

I always dream the same dream. I even dream in installments. It has to do with the lion.

Sometimes I dream I'm the lion himself, dreaming he's human. Funnily enough, I dream that in black and white.

Back then is always black and white to me.

CHAPTER TWO

The place where I am, *back then*, is a town called Kaulbach. The cobblestones bothered me at first, because of my crutch. When it's been raining, your crutch can easily slip away from under you on cobblestones.

I go down the street leading from the marketplace to school. I know what's going to happen next. I know because I've often had this dream before, but it still hurts every time. They'll be waiting for me behind the Owl pub. The town hall's on my left, and the old pub juts out into the street on my right. They're waiting behind the Owl. Waiting for me. I know them, because they're in my class at school: Fritz, Walter, and Paul.

"Ssh!" they hiss. "Here he comes!"

And I have to go past them. Then they jump out, shouting, "Heil Hitler, Your Majesty! Greetings to the lion of Kauba!"

"What's the big idea?" I say, but somehow they don't seem to understand me. Even I can hear that the words sound all choked as they come out, as if I'm retching. I can't speak very clearly, but I understand everything.

Then Walter says, "Oh, come on, Hannes, don't be a spoilsport! We only want you to roar for us! Do us the King of the Beasts!"

My name is Hannes in the dream.

I manage to get out a few strangulated words. "Leave me alone!"

But that doesn't stop them. "Yeah, sure, just as soon as you've done us your lion act." That was Paul.

"He's not going to do it on his own," says Fritz. "You have to kick his crutch away."

And next moment my crutch is lying in the road, and I'm roaring at the top of my voice. "Ow, ouch, ouch! Stop it, stop it!"

"That's more like it—listen to the lion of Kauba roaring, making the plains quiver! It gives all the blacks goose bumps!"

"Give me back my crutch!" I say, choking.

"Pick it up yourself!" says Fritz.

But I can't. I want to run away but I can't move from the spot. I stagger, I fall down. And then, at last, I hear *her*. "Leave Hannes alone!" she shouts. "Leave him alone, all of you!"

Now Paul and Fritz and Walter make

themselves scarce. "Watch out, here comes Hilde!" And they're off.

That's the good part of this dream— I have a girlfriend in it. Her name's Hilde Rosenbaum and she's in my class. She even sits next to me.

She helps me to my feet, dusts off my pants, retrieves the crutch, and gently pushes me forward. "Come on! Got everything? Hurry up, the others are already in class!"

When I emerge from the dream at this point, ten seconds at the most have passed. I've been miles away, as my mother says. It just suddenly happens to me now and then, even at mealtimes. I hold my full spoon suspended in midair, and the soup's still hot when I come out of the dream again. So it can't have lasted more than ten seconds. And when I feel carefully for my crutch, it's still leaning against my chair. My mother, noticing, sighs.

Time's different in the dream, although perhaps we can't ever really understand what time is anyway.

The ten seconds or less that passed while I was dreaming take more than twenty minutes in the dream itself. In the dream, I know Hilde and I are going to be late. The bell's already rung in the school yard, which is empty. The flight of steps leading to the school door is broad, flanked by two little walls, and the steps go up to the main entrance with the small staff entrance door beside it. Two large chestnut trees grow on the side of the yard next to the street, and the war memorial to those who fell in the world war stands in the yard too, in the middle.

We're going to be late anyway.

"Oh, do come on! What's the matter?"

I've stopped. I see something. "Look!"

Hilde sees it too, and immediately drags me behind one of the little walls flanking the steps.

"Duck down! And hold your breath, Lion!"

She calls me Lion, and I seem to like it, but I don't stop to think about that in the dream. I see two men in trench coats coming down the steps. I can see them even though I've ducked down behind the little wall. For a horrifying moment I realize that my crutch is sticking up above the wall, but I tell myself not to worry, because I'm only dreaming.

The two men are leading another man down the steps. It's Maximilian Goldstein, our math teacher. He's protesting. "Look, at least let me make a phone call!"

"Now then, Mr. Goldstein," says one of

the Gestapo men, "please don't give us any trouble!"

"But what have I done? I fought for my country! I fought at Verdun!"

He certainly did. He was always telling us about his wartime experiences. If we didn't feel like a math lesson, someone only had to feed him the right cue, and math would be over for the day. Old Gold Max would be off on the subject of the world war again.

But the soldiers don't even pretend to be interested that he once fought for Germany. The second Gestapo man says quietly, almost soothingly, "You're Jewish, Maximilian Goldstein. You're Jewish—that's enough, isn't it? Now, are you coming quietly, or do we have to . . . ?"

No, they don't. They push Goldstein into their car and close the doors, which open at the front, as if you could catch someone in the car that way while driving along full speed. The car starts off. Not too fast. Not too slow. Absolutely normal. Hilde and I are still crouching behind the little wall, but even so, I saw everything perfectly.

I never see more clearly and keenly than I do in the dream.

CHAPTER THREE

"Get up, they've gone," says Hilde.

"What will they do to him?" I hear my-self asking. But of course I know what they'll do. I've seen the pictures in our history book, and there was that film I saw about the concentration camps.

Driven up the ramp—guards yelling, "Get

a move on!"—the yards, the huts, the gas ovens, the electric fences . . . I know all about that in real life, but in the dream I don't know whether I know it or not. In Hilde's own real life, however, she seems to know something too.

She dismisses my question. "Don't ask! You didn't hear anything, you didn't see anything, understand? Come on, we have to get to class—oh, do hurry up!"

I do as she says. And a thought comes into my head: She's Jewish—that's enough, isn't it?

I don't know how we got up the steps to our classroom, all I remember is the smell, that typical school corridor smell.

Hilde's waiting for me. "Ready? Come on, then!" She opens the door.

The class jumps to its feet, stands to attention, and shouts in chorus, "Heil Hitler, Dr. Goldstein!"

On the word *Goldstein*, however, the chorus

falters. They've seen that it's only me and Hilde.

"Where's Old Gold Max?"

"Hey, no math today! Suits me!"

"What took you two so long?" asks Paul, appearing all innocent.

Fritz sings out, right on cue, "Luurve . . . sweet luurve!"

Everyone laughs. In the dream I blush, because they're right. I really do like Hilde Rosenbaum. I like her a lot. It's a shame I can't bring her back with me out of my dream. She's real there, but not here.

Being able to remember that I'm dreaming while I'm still in the dream helps me in both places. When I'm awake, I know I can go into the dream, and it isn't really dangerous.

And when I'm dreaming, it's a relief to be able to remember, for a split second, that I'm only dreaming, and I can escape from my dream anytime I want. But sometimes when I'm in it, I forget to be certain I'm dreaming, and then I shout something out loud.

I'm not shouting now, though. It's Karl, our class spokesman, standing at the door, who utters a loud yell. "Watch out!"

Then we're all on our feet at our desks, chanting, "Heil Hitler, sir!"

It's the headmaster. He says just, "Good morning."

Karl, ever the eager beaver, says, "Class Ten-B all present, sir."

The headmaster nods. We can sit down again. Once everyone is settled, he tells us, "I have an announcement to make: There'll be no math today."

Cheerful confusion breaks out. The headmaster clears his throat and says, "Dr. Goldstein has unexpectedly left the school."

His voice sounds husky and unconvincing. The word *left* is not exactly a lie, but it's not the whole truth either. "Your new math teacher will be Dr. Wilhelm Lang, coming to us from Berlin. Unfortunately, he won't be able to take up his post until the day after tomorrow." He stops and seems to be thinking something over. "Very well. What subject is your next lesson?"

"Physics, sir," says Karl.

"Then stay here in your classroom and do some physics preparation. You're the class spokesman?"

"Yes, sir!" Karl stands to attention.

"Right, I want you to make sure there's peace and quiet. I won't tolerate any clowning around, is that clear?"

"Yes, sir!"

"Oh, and one more thing." The headmaster turns back to face us again. "Two pupils came into this classroom only just before I did, obviously late for the lesson. Who were they? Well? Come on, I asked you a question!"

Karl says nothing.

No one else says anything either.

I see myself rising with difficulty from my seat, which folds up under me. Hilde Rosenbaum is already on her feet. "Me, sir," she says.

I hear myself stammering, also with difficulty, "And m-m-me, sir."

He says, "Well, I can understand it in your case, Hannes Keller." Hannes Keller, that's my full name in the dream. The name down in the class roll book. But I don't stop to think about that, I just take it for granted. Suddenly the headmaster is saying, in an unusually sharp voice, "But in *your* case, Miss Rosenbaum, I see no reason to make allowances!"

I'm horrified. I try to say something but I can't get it out.

"Miss Rosenbaum has two perfectly good legs," says the headmaster, turning to me. Then he turns to Hilde again. "Two good legs that could get you to the classroom in time for lessons, just like everyone else. What can you say by way of excuse, Hilde Rosenbaum?"

Hilde says nothing, just as she'd told me to say nothing. "You didn't hear anything, you didn't see anything." She keeps her own mouth shut.

The headmaster sighs. "No excuses, I see. You will come back to my office with me, and I shall enter a black mark against your name and give you a letter for your parents. As I said, I won't tolerate any discipline problems!"

I begin stammering again. Hilde leaves her desk without a word and follows the headmaster out of the room. I sit down at my desk.

At the same time I feel as if I were hovering above the rest of the class. Right at this moment I can see myself from outside as well as inside.

Karl is standing at the teacher's desk, shouting, "Quiet!"

Fritz leans over to Walter and whispers, "The Lion's blubbering!"

"Maybe it was all too much for him," Walter whispers back. "Hilde will comfort him!"

"Suppose Hilde tells on us."

"Don't be stupid!" hisses Walter.

"Or the Lion?"

"Should have thought of that before, shouldn't you?"

"Quiet at the back there!" shouts Karl.

"Show-off!" says Fritz under his breath, so that Karl can't hear it.

I see myself sitting at my desk, my head buried in my arms, crying, shedding silent tears.

The odd thing is that there are tears in my eyes in both worlds—in the dream and in real life. Mother told me so. When I start crying in the dream, she wakes me, because I really *am* crying. The tears that spring to my eyes in the dream world fall from them in real life. When Hannes cries, I cry too.

Mother thinks I take it all too much to heart.

As for Father, he's always saying, "Next parents' night I'm going to ask why they have to go unloading that dark chapter in our history on the children, of all people!"

But he never does ask.

My dream is like an invisible net.

It has to be pulled tight if it's to catch the truth. The more precise the questions I ask, the tighter the net will be.

My questions are like threads held in my hand, and the threads are not long enough yet.

I have to know more about what happened *back then*.

I have to tie up all the details.

But suppose I get caught in the net my-self. Suppose I entangle myself in it and can't escape again.

Everything in my dream has something to do with me.

I hold the threads in my hand, but nowhere near all of them. My net is drifting in the sea of oblivion.

There's nothing in that sea; it's been fished empty.

A dead sea, you might call it.

CHAPTER FOUR

I go and look in the library. I find documen-
tation: pictures and diaries. They're not
borrowed very often. Mother thinks it's a bad
idea for me to dwell on the gloomy, depress-
ing things that happened *back then*. I have
enough problems of my own to cope with,
she says.

She doesn't know I want to see Hilde again.

The more I read, the more I look at the pictures, the better the details fit together.

Unfortunately, they're all in black and white.

In my dreams, *back then* is always black and white.

I don't know why. I mean, they'd already had color films around for quite a long time. But I can't seem to see *back then* in color. My other world is black and white. Hilde's world, Hannes Keller's world.

I hate the idea that it must really have been in color.

Dreams are made of something. They're like an echo. I'm an echo-sounder. I send out my signals and dreams come back. The more I know about the world *back then*, the clearer my pictures are. I don't want to go on just dreaming the same thing over and over again.

I know a lot of the details. I can see the Rosenbaum family's house, with the garden behind it and the high cast-iron fence. I know what a wireless radio looks like *back then*, and I know what a better-quality radio set looks like too. The dream can go on to the next installment.

Mother asked what the matter was. I suddenly seemed so cheerful, she said. She doesn't like me to be cheerful; she's afraid when I've been on a high like that I'll fall back into the dark hole and wake in terror, weeping. What dark hole? I'm going to see Hilde again!

"Eat up, dear!" says Mother.

"Suppose he doesn't want to," Father objects.

I want to be alone.

I took the books back to the library when the loan period was up. The librarian said there wasn't really any great hurry, hardly anyone wanted to borrow books about all that these days. She asked if it was for school I needed them.

I nodded.

Now I'm lying on my bed, alone. At last. I stare at the ceiling. If I can keep it up long enough, at some point the pictures will emerge from that whitewashed ceiling. I only have to go on staring long enough. The ceiling responds. It's all starting up again as usual. The album. The lion. The street. The Gestapo. The headmaster saying good morning, and Hilde leaving the classroom in silence. Because she knows something, something that I know I ought not to have seen or heard myself.

In the dream I can be on both sides of

a door at the same time. Hilde is standing outside the door of her parents' sitting room. The door is closed, but her parents are in there, listening intently to their radio. It's not a wireless, it's one of the radio sets of better quality. The graduated gauge showing the radio stations glows amber.

Hilversum. Frankfurt. London.

A thin, bright green thread of light runs from top to bottom of the gauge, dividing it. The thread of light intersects the tiny box behind the word *London*.

The English news is struggling against a surging, rushing sea of confused voices and strange sounds made by static interference. The announcer's words fade away, disappear, and then emerge sharp and clear from the chaos of incomprehensible noise. Hilde knocks. "May I come in?"

Her mother turns off the radio. She shifts

the station indicator away from London. Then she calls out loud, in the direction of the doorway, "How many times do I have to tell you not to disturb us when we're having our midday rest?"

Hilde just says, "It's important."

Dr. Rosenbaum exchanges a swift glance with his wife. She nods. Hilde's father goes to the door and opens it. Hilde goes in, closes the door behind her, stands there and says, "They've taken Dr. Goldstein away."

"Maximilian?"

"They picked him up at school this morning."

"How do you know?"

"I saw it. I was late for class because the boys had taken the Lion's crutch away from him again. It was just after the bell rang. They came out of the staff entrance and they took him away with them."

"Oh, my God! Did anyone see you?" asks Hilde's mother, horrified.

"No, we ducked down behind the little wall there."

"Then what?"

Hilde shrugs her shoulders. "Well, we were late. The headmaster noticed right away. Here—you're supposed to sign this. He says he won't tolerate any discipline problems."

Hilde gives her father the envelope. It's a "blue letter": the bad conduct note they send your parents. Hesitantly, Hilde asks, "Well, will you sign it?"

"Was it really because of the Lion you were late?"

"Yes, of course. I said so!"

"Very well—we'll talk later."

"Thanks," says Hilde, relieved. She stands on tiptoe and kisses her father's throat. "See you, then."

While Hilde goes to her own room, Dr. Rosenbaum looks at the envelope and says, "He's never done that before."

"Done what?" asks Mrs. Rosenbaum.

"Sent a bad conduct note just because Hilde was late to class. I mean, he knows she helps the Lion."

Dr. Rosenbaum opens the envelope, unfolds the sheet of notepaper inside, frowns, and says, "I might have known. This isn't a bad conduct note, it's a letter. Oh, wait—yes, there's a small form too. That must be the note."

"What does he say?"

"Here, see for yourself."

Dr. Rosenbaum hands his wife the sheet of notepaper, and waits until she's read the letter.

I know what the letter says. I'm reading it through Mrs. Rosenbaum's eyes, and as I do so, I hear our headmaster's voice saying just

"Good morning!" when everyone's supposed to say "Heil Hitler!" instead.

Dear Dr. and Mrs. Rosenbaum,

I have given your daughter a black mark for bad conduct. I know she doesn't deserve it, but it was the only excuse I could find to write you this letter.

Maximilian Goldstein was taken away by the Gestapo this morning. They came for him in the staff room. You will know what that means. He hardly resisted at all, and there was no more I could do to help him. Would you please let his family know? And do be careful yourselves.

They have appointed a man from Berlin over my head to keep an eye on me, a Dr. Wilhelm Lang. There will be nothing more I can do for you now. They'll have your daughter expelled from school simply for being Jewish. When you have read this letter, please burn it. I never wrote it, and you never received it. And would you mind signing the enclosed form about your daughter Hilde being late for class? That will tell me that you've read this. I don't want to arouse suspicion, even in the office.

My very good wishes.

It can't be stopped now.

Mrs. Rosenbaum looks up from the letter. "He's a good man. A thoroughly decent man."

Dr. Rosenbaum nods. "But he won't be able to stand the strain much longer. This Dr. Lang from Berlin is only the start. Is there any fire left in the stove?"

"Let me see." Mrs. Rosenbaum goes over to the stove and opens the door. "Enough for the letter."

Dr. Rosenbaum throws the letter on the glowing embers. He doesn't close the stove door until the sheet of notepaper curls up underneath a bright flame, then falls in a black curve of ash, smolders, and fades away. Everything fades away: the paper, the writing on it, the news it brought, the anxieties of a decent man.

Out of the curve of ash and its faintly glowing edges, a room opens up. I know that room; it's our classroom. I'm always surprised by the way one picture in the dream grows out of another. I'm amazed to find how quickly I've arrived at school from the Rosenbaums' house. Time and distance shrink in the dream. They don't exist, everything is here and now.

CHAPTER FIVE

Where is Hilde Rosenbaum?

I have no time to think about that just now.

I see myself at my desk. The seat beside me is empty. I see myself, and I'm also inside myself looking out. Karl is standing by the door.

"Watch oooout!"

We all get to our feet. I know who's going to come in. "Heil Hitler, Dr. Lang!"

"Heil Hitler. Sit down."

Is this Dr. Lang in my dream really a Nazi? He looks more like a Boy Scout. Quite young, short haircut, watchful eyes. He does wear boots, yes. His voice sounds firm and clear. That's all right; he's leaving no one in any doubt about who's the teacher around here. I like him, although I really ought to hate him. How do I know that already?

"Anyone absent?" asks Dr. Lang, opening the roll book.

"Hilde Rosenbaum," says Karl.

Without looking up from the book, Dr. Lang says in a patient, long-suffering tone, "Now, how should you really have phrased it, Karl?"

Karl jumps up, stands at attention, and barks out, "Please, sir, I have to report that the pupil Sarah Hilde Rosenbaum is absent from school today, sir!"

Dr. Lang makes his entry in the book, apparently without much interest. "And why is that the case, Karl?"

Poor old Karl is puzzled. "I don't know, sir."

Smiling, Dr. Lang looks up from the roll book. "No, no—I mean I want to know why it's correct to say *Sarah* Hilde Rosenbaum."

I could have told Karl. I read about it in the books I borrowed from the library. But Karl doesn't need my help; he knows anyway. He's top of the class as well as class spokesman. "Because—because Jews have to have Jewish first names. Any Jews with non-Jewish first names must take another name too."

Karl is visibly relieved.

"And those first names are . . . ?" asks Dr. Lang.

"Sarah for Jewesses and Israel for Jews!" Karl was obviously ready for that one.

"Quite right," says Dr. Lang, nodding, satisfied. "Sit down!" Karl sits.

Dr. Lang puts his fountain pen away and closes the roll book. "So, why did the pupil Sarah Hilde Rosenbaum not come to school today? And why won't she be coming to school tomorrow or the day after tomorrow either? Well, who can tell me the answer?"

Dr. Lang looks inquiringly around the class.

I'm horrified. Not because Dr. Lang's eyes rest on me for a fraction of a second—I'm horrified because Hilde won't be sitting next to me tomorrow, or the day after tomorrow either. How did I know about that? Where did I read it? And—why was I surprised and horrified to hear it now? Had I suppressed it somehow? Of course Hilde couldn't come to school anymore. That was the law. I knew about it from my books, but I didn't want this to happen.

My dream is stronger than what I want, though.

I'm horrified at myself, because after all, it's me dreaming all this.

I hear Dr. Lang ask again, "Well, who can tell me?" I almost put my hand up, because I know about the new regulations.

"No one?" says Dr. Lang. "Then *I* will tell *you* why: Jews are not allowed to attend German schools."

Now the others know too. Most of them are staring down at their desks, looking awkward. Dr. Lang seems rather disappointed in us. There is a slight touch of reproach in his voice when he adds, "And because it's high time we took the Führer's laws as seriously in this school as anywhere else."

Well, I know who that was intended for! I can guess. Now that I've dreamed the letter to the Rosenbaums, it gives Lang's remark a meaning, a purpose, a context. I'm much more logical in the dream than I am in waking life. I know that Lang will be making some kind of move against the headmaster. At the same time, I feel that a dream that threatens Hilde must threaten me too. Am I just thinking that to get out of my role as a patriotic German boy? Am I dreaming it because I'd rather be a victim than a hanger-on?

Maybe I have to hang on to a crutch, but I don't have to be the other kind of hanger-on. I realize I'm beginning to divide myself up, split myself. I have to see this through as Hannes Keller. But I'm not entirely submerged in Hannes. As long as I can still wonder in the dream where I get this sense of the urgency of events from, I can protect myself. In the dream I don't think about it, but I know I *am* thinking about it all the same. . . .

Dr. Lang interrupts my thoughts. He's about to call on me. He says, "Today we're going to tackle some arithmetic exercises based on real life. Exercises showing us the problems facing the Führer in Berlin, the capital of our Reich; problems he has to solve for the good of the whole people. Now, who shall we have up at the blackboard today? Yes, well, why not—come up here, Hannes Keller!"

I see myself stand up. I have difficulty disentangling my crutch from the desk, where it's gotten stuck in my folding seat. Finally I get it under my arm and limp up to the blackboard. Dr. Lang looks at me, eyebrows raised. At close quarters he seems tougher, not so youthful anymore. He's obviously getting impatient over the time it takes me to reach the board. You don't keep someone like Dr. Lang waiting and get away with it.

"So, you're Hannes Keller. And you live in . . . ?"

I hear my wretched, strangulated "Ka-u-ba!" emerge. "Where?" asks Dr. Lang, as if he hadn't heard correctly. I have to make the effort all over again. "Kaaah-uuu-baaach!"

The others giggle. They know I can't pronounce *Kaulbach*. *Kauba* sounds African. It sounds like lions.

"Quiet, please!" Dr. Lang inspects me. "Hannes Keller. Lives in Kaulbach. Father civil servant, mother housewife." He runs off this information almost in passing, as if he needed to remind himself of it. Just in case. Well, just in this particular case. I'm a case, and he's collecting information for my case history. "Very well, write on the board as I dictate!"

Then he reads the exercises out loud. He reads them, and I write them on the board in chalk. At least, I try to. I have to keep my balance at the same time. I press too hard on the chalk, and it squeaks as it crosses the blackboard. I feel I'm going too slowly for him, since he goes on steadily dictating. "'According to conservative estimates, there are three hundred thousand mentally ill patients, epileptics, cripples, and so forth in institutional care in Germany. a) What do these people cost annually, in all, given expenses of four Reichsmarks a day per person? b) How many low-interest government loans of one thousand Reichsmarks each could be made per year to young married couples with the same sum of money?'"

I've only just reached *epileptics* when Dr. Lang begins dictating the second exercise: "'Building a lunatic asylum costs six million Reichsmarks. How many council houses, each costing fifteen hundred Reichsmarks, could be built for the same sum of money?'"

Only now does Dr. Lang look up, and

I see myself standing there at the board, still struggling with the word *epileptics.*

"Got that? For heaven's sake, Keller, don't stand there like a half-wit, get it on the board: 'According to conservative estimates, there are three hundred thousand mentally ill patients, epileptics, cripples, and so forth in institutional care in Germany. What do these people cost annually, in all, given expenses of four Reichsmarks a day per person?' Oh, come on, Keller! Surely you should know how to spell *epileptics?*"

The chalk snaps in my fingers. I give up. I just stand there, trying to keep my balance by leaning on my crutch. I begin working out the exercise in my head. Dr. Lang goes on dictating. I do some mental arithmetic:

One cripple costing 365 times 4 a year makes 1,460 Reichsmarks, so all the cripples cost 1,460 times 300,000: times three, add five zeros, that comes to 438 million Reichs-marks in all . . .

Dr. Lang is dictating. "'Building a lunatic asylum costs . . .'" At the word *costs* he inter-rupts himself. "Who was whispering? Who gave the answer?"

No one speaks up.

Walter whispers, "The Lion's in for it now!" Paul nods. Finally he stands up and says, "Dr. Lang, sir, the Lion, I mean Hannes, well, he can't do sums so well on the board, see?"

"He can't? What do you mean, he can't?"

Walter speaks up. "It's because of his paralysis, and the crutch, and anyway the Lion does sums like that in his head!"

But Walter hasn't mollified Dr. Lang. "In his head? In his head? I'll pretend I didn't hear that! And I don't see anything on the board. I only hear two pupils trying to whisper him the answer out of some mistaken notion of comradeship, and then they have the impudence to interrupt their teacher! Where do you think we are? Is this a madhouse or a good German school?"

It suddenly bursts out of me: "Four hundred and thirty-eight million Reichsmarks, four hundred and thirty thousand low-interest government loans, and four thousand council houses."

But it sounds terrible. Everything I say is gummed up with saliva. I get the words out like a bird bringing up pellets, my mouth and my tongue won't obey me, but it's the answer I worked out in my head.

Dr. Lang looks at me in silence.

Walter takes his silence as a request for information. "'Scuse me, Dr. Lang, sir, but that *was* the answer."

For a moment Lang loses control of himself. "Are you trying to make fun of me, boy?"

And Walter, who seems to be standing up for me all of a sudden, says in a subdued voice, "No, Dr. Lang, sir—it's just that Hilde, who usually sits next to him, I mean Sarah Hilde Rosenbaum, she understands him better than anyone else, and she used to tell people what he was saying. But now—"

Dr. Lang bellows, "How dare you? I don't want to hear another word about that Jewish girl. She won't be sitting next to him anymore! She's been removed from the roll book for good! Why do you think I explained it all to you a moment ago?"

And as if the crutch wanted to answer for me, it slips away and I fall over. Dr. Lang controls himself again. He takes a deep breath, as if he'd seen all this coming, and he tells me, in tones of weary patience, "Kindly stop playing for sympathy and get up!"

I can't, and perhaps I don't want to either. Walter tries again. "Dr. Lang, sir—" But he gets no further. Dr. Lang is back in command of himself. Smiling, he says, "Well, if anyone here expects me to fall for feebleness of mind disguised as something clever, he can think again. Come along, Keller, get up! Schumann, you help him! How much longer will this go on? Are we about to waste the entire lesson fooling around with a crutch? Brigit Schuster—what's *your* answer to the problem?"

And as Paul helps me up and I limp back to my desk, I hear Brigit Schuster giving the answers I'd worked out myself.

"The three hundred thousand cripples, epileptics, and mentally ill people cost the German Reich four hundred thirty eight million Reichsmarks a year in all. The same sum of money would pay for four hundred thirty-eight low-interest government loans to young married couples. And the six million Reichsmarks it costs to build a lunatic asylum would pay for four thousand new council houses at fifteen hundred Reichsmarks each."

I know these arithmetic exercises. I read them in a school textbook from *back then*. I opened it at those pages by chance, not that I believe in chance anymore. Those exercises were invented specially for me. Arithmetic exercises based on real life, just waiting for someone like me. Made for me—well, made *against* me. At this moment Hannes is standing outside our front door. He's digging around in his pants pocket with one hand to find his key. I can hear my mother calling from the kitchen. "Hannes—Hannes, is that you?" Then she's standing in the doorway in front of me. I can't utter a word. She looks at me as if she didn't recognize me. "Hannes? Hannes! What happened to you? For heaven's sake, dear—you look so pale! Say something, Hannes! Hannes!"

I don't say anything. I can't make a sound. The part of me that's really *me* and not Hannes, that part of me has been struck dumb by my sudden realization that the Kellers' house is *our* house.

Although we don't live in Kaulbach, it's our house, all right. And although Hannes's mother can't be my mother, it's still my mother letting me in at the door and begging, "Oh, say something! Do say something!"

I can't stay here in this dream. I have to wake up to reassure myself that I really do still exist.

My mother is holding my chin. She keeps on whispering. "Say something, dear, speak to me!"

Finally my convulsions wear off. I've bitten my tongue so hard, I almost choked.

CHAPTER SIX

I don't want to be back in that dream. I go out in the fresh air more often these days, although it's very tiring for me. My tongue has healed again. I don't like lying in bed in the middle of the day staring at the ceiling.

Father's noticed I seem to look at Mother

differently now. He thinks it's just a normal development of puberty. He has no idea what's occupying my mind. Why did I take my mother into that dream with me? Do I need her protection?

And what about him, my father?

I don't think I really want to know. But if I don't want to know, why does it bother me? Saying I don't *really* want to know can't be true.

Mother says she heard me choking, and we had to protect my tongue because of the convulsions. It was bad enough thinking she might *not* have heard me, she says. Father says I've gotten worse since we started studying "that subject" in school. He's finally going to have it out with the teachers, he says. But he never does.

I got an A at school for my essay about *back then*. I'd put in a bit about the exercises I worked out in the dream.

I found myself getting out the old album of photos again. With the picture of the dying lion. We looked at each other for a long time. That lion doesn't really have much of a chance against a human being. The lion has something to do with Hannes. But he has something to do with me too.

Once, when I was only little, I liked lying in bed in the morning. I wanted to go on dreaming right to the end of the dream.

Now I know there are dreams you can't just switch off. I used to be sorry I couldn't get back into my dreams. Now I'm afraid of what's sure to happen next. My dream is a fantasy catching the truth. An invisible net, and I'm caught in it myself and struggling.

Fresh air makes you tired.

I'm hardly lying down on my bed before the dream is back. Everyone's present except for Maximilian Goldstein. I'm in the staff room. I don't know what a staff room would have looked like *back then*, but I do know for sure this has to be one.

All the teachers in the school are listening to a man speaking calmly, in almost matter-of-fact tones. It's Dr. Lang, and he's talking about me. Now I know why I'm here. Does he guess I'm listening to him this very minute?

"My dear colleagues, I will repeat it: The boy ought to be in an institution. A useful member of society, a national comrade? Not a hope of it, not him. He may even be an epileptic; you should have seen him standing up there at the blackboard. I think I may say, in fact, I think I *must* say, among ourselves, that it simply will not do for our young German citizens of the future, boys and girls from healthy families who are ready and willing to study, to be held back by such a creature's slowness and infirmity. Hannes Keller should be in a home."

He speaks in a down-to-earth way, as if the idea was the most natural thing in the world. After that long, highly polished bit leading up to it he just says, briefly: Hannes Keller should be in a home. Full stop.

It's very clever. He can use words. He knows that a short sentence after a long one comes as a relief, a respite. It sounds purposeful, factual, decisive.

Only the headmaster objects. "I can't agree, Dr. Lang. In spite of his handicaps, Hannes Keller's considered a bright boy. He's particularly strong in mathematics. You should take a look at his grades!"

But a man like Lang doesn't give in so easily. Smiling, he tosses a question back. "And who, Headmaster, who gave him those grades? Wasn't it a certain Maximilian Goldstein? I have to ask myself, in all seriousness, where would we be if we were to give credence to the false humanity of a Jew, a parasite on society, long after he has been removed from the staff of this school?

"I tested the boy myself. There's nothing there. And I suggest that you do not fall retrospectively for the ruses of an impertinent Jewish girl who pretended to understand his strangulated speech. She used to claim he said things that he never *could* have said or thought. You know the girl I mean."

Yes, the staff knows. Some of them nod.

Only the headmaster shows some backbone. "Dr. Lang, I must insist on expressing my doubts of your appraisal."

That was clear enough. It'll have to go down in the minutes of the staff meeting.

Not that Dr. Lang seems much impressed.

"And your doubts do you great credit, Headmaster. Yes, such doubts are essential in the search for a truly humane attitude. But what exactly are we doubting?

"Let's look at the law imposed by the creator of this world on his creation, and on our lives: it is the harsh, indeed the brutal law of the struggle for survival, and of selection in that struggle. Anything that cannot stand up to the great demands made on it will break—however much that hurts! Are we, in an excess of humanity and misguided pity, to give the sick precedence over the young, strong, and healthy, the rising generation?

"The youth of Germany faces tasks of truly great magnitude. May we all do our duty.

"Heil Hitler!"

The silence in the staff room now is tacit agreement. They'll do their duty; that was all Dr. Lang wanted.

The rest of it's a pure formality.

"Well, colleagues," says Dr. Lang, "I have proposed a motion. May we have a show of hands? Which of those present is in favor of getting in touch with the medical officer of health and applying for the pupil Hannes Keller to be transferred to a home?

"Thank you. Votes against?

"None. Abstentions?"

"Yes. I abstain," says the headmaster gravely.

"Then the motion is carried unanimously, with one abstention."

CHAPTER SEVEN

What did I expect? Unanimously. One
abstention. Hasn't the headmaster gotten
himself into enough trouble just by abstain-
ing? Did I really want him to make himself
vulnerable to a character like Lang?

Didn't I know, from the books I'd read,
that *back then* a good many parents them-

selves were glad to be relieved of such a "burden" by their child's school, by the medical officer of health, by the family doctor?

Well, all I really knew was that I was the burden.

Could my mother *back then* have been the same as my mother now? And what about my father, who's always intending to "do something about" this or that, and never does?

It's a funny thing, but I can't seem to focus on what my father looks like in the dream. Not yet, anyway. I always see my mother instead. Now she's standing at the door to the veranda looking out on the Rosenbaums' garden. It's still closed. What's my mother doing at the Rosenbaums' house? Why is she approaching from the back, across the garden and over the veranda?

She doesn't want anyone to see her. Cautiously, she knocks on the pane of the sash window.

"Dr. Rosenbaum? Dr. Rosenbaum!"

She's whispering.

"Dr. Rosenbaum!"

At last there's a quiet answer from inside. "Who is it?"

"It's me. Else Keller."

Now the veranda door opens, just a narrow crack. "Mrs. Keller? In the middle of the night? Come in—please, come in. Mind you don't fall over the suitcases. My wife meant to put them away long ago."

That last sentence sounds very awkward, as if it had been carefully rehearsed in advance.

"Did anyone see you?"

"No," says my mother. "I came through the garden."

This seems to reassure Dr. Rosenbaum. "Does your husband know you're here?"

"No, I didn't tell him."

"Good. But please sit down—can I do

anything for you?" Dr. Rosenbaum is very much the family doctor again.

"I need your advice," says Mother. "It's about Hannes."

"Is he unwell? Has he injured himself?"

"No," says Mother, "but we've had a letter. From the medical officer of health. Hannes is to go into a home. It's for his own good, they say, and we're supposed to sign a consent form. I don't want to. And you know my Hannes—if anyone knows him, you do! He's handicapped, yes, but he's bright and he has a lovely nature. So why put him in a home? The medical officer's pressing us for an answer, and there's a deadline. Oh, what am I to do? I just don't know—I really don't know what to do!"

My mother is near tears.

Dr. Rosenbaum does not answer immediately. He seems to be wondering how much he ought to tell my mother. He seems to know more than he says. And he doesn't appear to like my father.

"Mrs. Keller," he says, "Mrs. Keller, if you love your son Hannes, then don't sign! No one knows exactly what goes on in those institutions, but there are some nasty rumors going around. Too many people die there. They've even built a crematorium in the institution at Grafeneck. Why would they do that, Mrs. Keller, if they didn't know there were going to be deaths there? And do you know how that news got out? The truck bringing the heavy incinerators from Berlin got stuck in the snow and had to be towed out, so now we know what it was carrying. Too late for some, but not too late for Hannes.

"And I'll tell you something else, Mrs. Keller. Buses arrive there daily, bringing far too many people for such a small place. Buses with whitewashed windows. They say the buses are full of mentally sick people who'd like to know where they're going, but they can't see anything because the windows are whitewashed over.

"When those buses drive through Urach, the women by the roadside cross themselves and the railway workers outside Münsingen take their caps off. They all know more than we do, but they're not allowed to talk about it. They're afraid. Rumors, that's all we have, but perhaps someday the whole truth will come out. Don't sign anything, Mrs. Keller. That's the best advice I can give you."

There's no sound now but the ticking of the clock on the wall. Dr. Rosenbaum is standing. My mother is sitting down. Neither of them says anything. When my mother at last gets to her feet she says, quietly, "Thank you, Doctor. I'll go back through the garden. I was never here tonight. And—and I didn't see anything. But I wish you a good journey. Good-bye!"

I am proud of my mother. I'm proud of her *back then*, just the way I'm proud of her today. I seem to be sitting in one of the two chestnut trees growing on one side of the school yard, and at the same time I can see myself standing underneath them. All alone.

CHAPTER EIGHT

Not far away from me, Fritz and Walter are strolling over the yard.

"Hey, look at that!" Fritz nudges Walter in the ribs.

"What?"

"The Lion, of course—he's fixed his crutch to his wrist with a leather strap now that there's no one to pick it up for him!"

"So? Not a bad idea."

"Won't do him any good, though. I'll bring my sheath knife to school tomorrow, and then—*swoosh!*"

"Oh, leave him alone," says Walter.

"Hey there!" Fritz sounds indignant. "What's eating you?"

"Nothing," says Walter.

"Now old Lang's said the Lion's fair game, you have to go and be a spoilsport!"

"For goodness' sake, will you shut up?"

But Fritz isn't letting go. "Come on, don't be like that! What's come over you all of a sudden?"

"I just don't like it anymore."

"You're just soft!"

And Fritz marches away. I'd have liked to fly down from the chestnut tree and settle on his shoulder, as a kind of sign. But now I'm in the classroom. They let me in early because it takes me longer with my crutch, and I need more time than other people to get anywhere. And then I'm not in the classroom or in the corridor outside it either; I'm not in the chestnut tree or in the school yard. I'm here in my bed, with the light out, but I'm not asleep yet. I don't know whether I'm lying awake or whether I'm dreaming, or maybe whether I'm dreaming that I'm lying awake.

I can hear my father outside at the front door. He's trying to open it, swearing to himself. "All these stupid locked doors!"

He's been drinking again.

My mother goes to open the door without a word.

It's been like this for the last three days. The same every evening.

Breathing heavily, he pushes himself away from the door frame and staggers into the hall. My mother closes the front door quickly. She's ashamed.

"The boy still here, is he?" asks my father, slurring his words. My mother didn't catch what he said.

"Oh, why do you have to do it?" she asks. "You've been drinking again! I can't understand you."

"So long as I'm earning our living, I suppose I can buy myself a beer."

My mother tries to help him out of his coat, but he resists. "Stop that. I can do it for myself. Have to do everything for myself anyway. Nobody's got the nerve to do anything around here. Still, someone has to sign things, and that means the head of the household."

"What do you mean, sign things?" Mother is suddenly hearing perfectly clearly. "You haven't signed anything I don't know about?"

"So what do you know? You don't know anything. Not a thing! Better that way!"

"Friedrich!" Mother sounds uncertain.

"Friedrich, tell me it's not true. You haven't signed anything. You've been drinking. You don't know what you're saying. Come into the bedroom and lie down. I'll take your shoes off. Come on!"

Suddenly Father is quiet as a lamb. He lets her propel him into the bedroom. He stretches out on the bed. I hear his shoes clatter as they fall to the wooden floor. Slowly, as if in a trance, I stand up. I'm fully dressed. I make my way to the door in my stockinged feet. Now I can hear them again. Their voices sound muffled, but I can hear everything: I want to hear it, I have to hear it.

"You're only trying to frighten me. Why do you do it? You do it every time you've been drinking."

And then come my father's slow, slurred words. "Four days ago. Four days ago I did it. Medical officer came to see me. Party member too. Hannes, going to a home. Better that way, better for him, better for us. You'll get some time to yourself then. Medical officer explained it all."

"Friedrich, stop it!"

But he doesn't stop it. "Know who gave them Hannes's name? The school. That's right, the school. Teacher called Dr. Lang. So the medical officer told me. He has to do what Lang says. That's why we got the letter. And no more child allowance either, seeing Hannes won't ever make a useful national comrade. It's official now."

Mother can't believe it. "Friedrich, you're drunk. You haven't signed anything—I know you, Friedrich. You wouldn't do a thing like that without telling me? Friedrich? I do know you, don't I?"

I'm not so sure that she really does.

"Interests of the individual have to come second to the interests of the nation as a whole, 's what the medical officer said. Or, my dear Keller, he said, do you want—do you want your family down in the files as suffering from hereditary disease? Hereditary disease, Else, hereditary disease, know what that means? Do you know? No, you don't know. But I know. I have to know. I work for the city. I'm not all that high up in the civil service, but I know what hereditary disease means: You can't get a loan. Lose your ranking in the department. End of everything. Yes, I signed, Else. Four days ago. They were going to come for him by now. 'S why I've been so late. Didn't want to have to watch. No. And yes, I've been drinking. That's why, Else. That's the only reason why."

And I hear my mother, in a thread of a voice, asking one question again and again. "Do you know what you're saying? Do—you—know—what—you're—saying?"

"Stop that!" cries my father. "Stop that! Stop it, will you?" I hear him bellowing like an injured ox, I hear the blows, I hear him repeating, "Stop it! Stop it!" over and over again.

I know he's beating my mother. He thinks he'll get her to see reason that way. He'll drive her out of her mind. I can't stand this. I feel the leather strap around my wrist, and the crutch. I close the front door after me. I need fresh air!

CHAPTER NINE

My way is already decided for me in the dream.

I go the same way as my mother.

I go through the garden.

I know what I'm going to tell her. "Hilde? It's happened. I've come to see you because I have to tell you something. My father's signed the form, and you can't go back to school either. Dr. Lang struck you out of the roll book. I saw it. He crossed out your name. So far as he's concerned you might as well be dead. Hilde, you must go away from here or they'll get you! Do you understand?

"Sarah Hilde Rosenbaum. Dr. Lang said you have to be called Sarah. Your name was still Hilde in the roll book, no Sarah in front of it, but it was crossed out. You have to go away, a long way away. And I have to go away too, though I don't know where."

Now I'm standing at the veranda door. I knock our special signal. I hear myself calling, "Hilde? Open the door! It's me, Hannes. Can't you hear me, Hilde?" Then the door handle gives. The door's not locked. I see myself slipping into the house as quickly as possible. I'm calling you. "Hilde? Hilde!"

But you don't answer. The grandfather

clock has stopped. I make my way upstairs to your room. "Hilde? Hilde!" No, I won't switch on a light. I strike a match. I can see you've left the room neat and tidy. Even your bed has clean sheets on it. You haven't slept in it, and your teddy bear's gone.

The match burns my fingers.

I have to strike another. Then I see the picture on your desk, with your crayons beside it. You've left me a picture. An ocean-going steamer, with *America* on the bows. There's already smoke coming out of the funnels, so it's about to sail away. And there's a rosebush growing out of the stern at the back, a rosebush with thorns and a single rose. The rose is on a very long stem, reaching right out and over the harbor wall. A lion is sitting there on the quayside, smelling it. Lions don't usually smell roses. Ouch!

Another match. He's a tame lion. He's

leaning on a crutch and dreaming. There are men standing behind him, but he can't see them.

That's it. No more matches.

I roll up the picture. I think how far away America is. And as I go slowly downstairs to the veranda door, as I feel the gravel of the garden path under my feet, I can't stop thinking of the lion. A lion on a crutch. The lion of Kauba. I think how real lions in the zoo prowl back and forth on the concrete floor of their cages until their paws bleed. Back and forth, back and forth. Then they limp. A limping lion looks kind of silly.

They ought to be let out of their cages, but of course that would be no good. In the wild, lions go into hiding when they're sick or injured.

I ought not to have fallen over at the blackboard. They catch lions in nets in Africa. The net has to be well hidden so the lion won't notice it. Then he struggles, and they give him a tranquilizer so he won't hurt himself, and when he wakes up, he's caught. In a cage, on a ship, crossing the sea. The ship disappears beyond the horizon.

When lions in the zoo get sick, or too old, they're put to sleep to spare them suffering. They get put to sleep with an injection, and their keeper cries.

I'm crying. My mother's crying. The doctor says the injection will calm me. I was terrified. I can take the gag out of my mouth again now. It was only there because of my tongue. I know I've woken up again. These convulsions are horrible, like a storm inside my head.

I know I've woken up, because *back then* it's always black and white, and now there's light and color around me. If there's a real Hilde Rosenbaum and she really is in

America, I'll write to her. And I'll paint a picture to go with the letter. With that thought in my mind I fall into a deep, dreamless sleep.

All this was some time ago now. I'm back here in the world of color all the time these days, but I think about it a lot.

My parents say they love me. I believe my mother when she says so. She loves me the way I am. I'm her only child. I don't have any brothers and sisters.

When I ask why I don't have a little brother or sister, tears come into my mother's eyes, and my father says I'm too young to understand. I know what it is: They're afraid of having another child like me.

When there are visitors, I usually go up to my room. Any visitors who want me to stay downstairs had better leave their sympathy outside at the door. Most of them are sorry for my parents. "What a lot you've been through with your boy." That sort of thing makes Mother feel ashamed.

Father doesn't mind, because then he can explain how he loves me all the same, and no amount of moaning will help; I'm here and that's that.

I don't want to be loved "all the same." And I don't want to be loved "in spite of" it, or "although," and most certainly not "all the more because" I'm the way I am.

Chapter Ten

I painted Hilde Rosenbaum's picture from memory, and now it's hanging over my bed. The lion of Kauba on the quayside, beside the ship with the rosebush in the stern. I managed to bring the picture home with me from *back then*.

And there's something else that's stayed

with me too—I can't bring myself to trust my father anymore. He doesn't know about my dream, but he can sense there's something not quite right between us. He puts it down to puberty.

Puberty is something he sees as quite normal, and he doesn't have to bother about anything normal.

When I think about it, I'm not so sure I could be born today. There's genetic testing now. They can test you for hereditary diseases, and if people who want to be parents have a defective gene, they're advised against having children of their own. That way a person like me wouldn't exist. Genetic testing won't let anyone but perfect human beings through.

But then where will the others be?

Back then I'd probably have been killed.

These days I ought not to exist at all.

But since I do exist, I'm a living reproach.

A living example of what won't have to happen in the future anymore.

Father is more ashamed of me than Mother is. I think Mother's ashamed because of the horrible way people sympathize with her.

I'm glad I exist! No one can argue me away. But I have a suspicion that Father's sorry these genetic tests weren't around *before* I was born.

He thinks that in the future they'll even be able to repair defective genes. What he doesn't say is that then I'll still be just the way I am now. He'd have liked me to be normal and complete, which you can maybe understand, but I'd never want to be like him! I'd rather be "defective."

There'll always be people worse off than me. And there always must have been, too. When I stop to think about *back then*, I wonder where *I* was before I was born.

Where exactly?

We can't imagine nothingness, or a vacuum, or infinity or eternity. It makes our heads swim.

But we must have been somewhere before we were born.

Perhaps that's why we believe we always existed and always will.

To me, God's a word for something we don't understand. And other words like that are a vacuum, nothingness, eternity and infinity. We cling to words we don't understand. Still, they save us from going crazy.

Anyone who says he can get his mind around the idea of God is lying. Or else he's God himself.

I guess I'll never be a devout believer.

I still have that collected album with the photo of the injured lion. *Adventures in Ger-*

man *South-West Africa*. The lion is a natural creature. Man has guns. All the same, if I were ever to come into the world again, I'd rather be a lion. With Hilde a lioness beside me. We'd be a very unusual couple of lions, both of us liking the scent of roses. Most lions don't.

And I'd be happy if there were really somewhere called Kauba in Africa.

Kauba is Africa.

But nothing at all makes me want to go to Kaulbach.

"Back then . . ."
THE BACKGROUND TO
HANNES KELLER'S STORY

The time to which the narrator goes back in his dream is the period of the Nazi Third Reich, when Adolf Hitler was in power in Germany.

It began in 1933, when President Hindenburg of the German Reich appointed Hitler as Chancellor of Germany. In the general elections of March 1933, the National Socialist Workers' Party (known as the Nazi party), with their allies the right-wing German National Party, won a majority in the Reichstag, the German parliament. Hitler and his National Socialists then attacked Poland and Russia, declared their aim of creating a "Greater Germany," and started World War II, which cost millions of lives. They had no scruples about attempting to exterminate all European Jews in the wave of persecutions now known as the Holocaust.

None of this would have been possible if the majority of Germans had not accepted the Nazi ideology and Adolf Hitler's aims in the first place.

Hannes's story focuses attention on another Nazi extermination campaign. It has not attracted much attention because its first victims were patients in mental hospitals and similar institutions for the disabled. And, even today, there is often a vague feeling that it is better for such people to be kept locked up, well away from the rest of the world.

THE IDEOLOGY, LAWS, AND PROPAGANDA

Hitler and his National Socialist Party aimed to create a "healthy" nation of people of German blood, members of what they regarded as the pure, superior Nordic race. These people were to be perfect Aryan human beings, ordained by "Providence" to rule the world.

The ideas about a master race of German

"supermen" put forward by Hitler and the Nazis implied that everyone else was subhuman. There was no place in their healthy nation for the weak, the sick, or those in need of care.

And the doctrine of the pure Aryan race would tolerate nothing foreign. Drawing up your frontiers means keeping people out as well as in. The state that believed Providence had chosen it to rule the world now set out on a process of selection. It was a process eventually leading to the murder of undesirable members of society. They were exterminated on a large scale, because theirs were considered "lives not worth living," a "dead weight," "useless mouths," and "racially inferior."

At that time, a boy like the narrator of this story would have been killed.

The National Socialists euphemistically referred to the murder of people whose lives were not worth living as *euthanasia* (a word taken from the ancient Greek and meaning "a good death") or *mercy killing*. These were fine-sounding words to describe dreadful crimes.

This first mass murder by the Nazis killed over two hundred thousand people by means of poison gas, sedative drugs, or deliberate starvation.

A number of laws prepared for the exclusion from ordinary society and ultimately the extermination of everyone who did not fit into the Nazis' idea of their "healthy national body," and legalized such actions.

Propaganda methods had to be used, to make most people think these laws were necessary. First, the families were made to feel ashamed of their disabled children or other relatives; there was a strong suggestion that they themselves were responsible for the disability.

Second, the propaganda machine took every opportunity of informing the "healthy German nation" of the huge expense and unfortunate consequences of showing any compassion to those who needed care. Calculations were constantly quoted to prove that the disabled were being supported at the expense of the healthy. The arithmetic exercise Hannes has to work out comes from a school textbook of the time.

Operation T4

The "elimination of lives not worth living" was planned and organized by an inconspicuous civil service office at No. 4 Tiergartenstrasse, Berlin. The operation took its name from the number of the building and the initial of the street.

This department for murder began its work in 1939 with a systematic survey of all the patients then in psychiatric institutions. By August 1941, those involved in Operation T4 had shown, within a very short time, that they had the organization and technology, the necessary staff and the administrative backup to handle the murder of over 70,000 people.

As a result, the same civil service department was told to carry out the second phase of the operation: gassing concentration camp inmates who were unable to work, exhausted, or disruptive.

The circle of people whose lives were regarded as "not worth living" was now extended to "social misfits." The victims this time were vagrants, petty thieves, chronic alcoholics, pimps, people who avoided paying alimony, and the generally antisocial, as well as everyone classified as "work-shy," meaning that they were no longer strong enough to be used for labor in the camps.

In the end, this "elimination of lives not worth living" turned out to be the model for the other terrible mass murders committed by the Nazis: The experience gleaned from their criminal "euthanasia" was put to the service of the "final solution of the Jewish problem," the Holocaust that swallowed up the Jews of Europe.

SOURCES

This book could not have been written without the earlier documentary work of Ernst Klee, whose book entitled *Euthanasie im NS-Staat—Die Vernichtung des lebensunwerten Lebens* (*Euthanasia in the Nazi State—The Elimination of Life Not Worth Living*) was published in Germany in 1983 by S. Fischer-Verlag, Frankfurt am Main.

The second book that helped me with my research is edited by Götz Aly and entitled *Aktion T4* (*Operation T4*). It appeared as volume 27 in a series on sites in the history of Berlin, published by Edition Hentrich, Berlin 1987.

It could have been these two books that the narrator studied in the present day to tighten his "invisible net" in order to catch the truth about the "elimination of lives not worth living."